SO-AJA-428

Dd Ee Ff

Jj Kk Ll

Pp Qq Rr

Vv Ww Xx

Yolanda

Yolanda's YELLOW SCHOOL

by Kelly Asbury

Henry Holt and Company
New York

Henry Holt and Company, Inc.
Publishers since 1866
115 West 18th Street
New York, New York 10011

Henry Holt is a registered trademark
of Henry Holt and Company, Inc.
Copyright © 1997 by Kelly Asbury
All rights reserved.
Published in Canada by Fitzhenry & Whiteside Ltd.,
195 Allstate Parkway, Markham, Ontario L3R 4T8.

Library of Congress Cataloging-in-Publication Data
Asbury, Kelly.
Yolanda's yellow school/Kelly Asbury.
Summary: Young Yolanda enjoys show-and-tell, reading,
finger painting, playing after lunch, and watching a
video during a day in first grade.
[1. Schools—Fiction.] I. Title.
PZ7.A775Yo 1996 [E]—dc20 96-21714

ISBN 0-8050-4023-4
First Edition—1997
Typography by Martha Rago
The artist used water-soluble crayon on bristol
board to create the illustrations for this book.
Printed in the United States of America
on acid-free paper.◁▷
10 9 8 7 6 5 4 3 2 1

For my mentors:
Minnie McMillan, Jerry Newman, and Lane Smith
—K. A.

My name is Yolanda.

I am in the first grade.

This morning for show-and-tell, Gretchen Gold brought her canary, Buttercup.

This is Mrs. Amberson.

She teaches us things like reading…

...and my favorite subject

finger painting!

It is my turn to feed the fish.

Not too much!

I get hungry, too. My mom always
packs me a good lunch. Just enough.

After we eat,
the playground becomes a busy place.

We all get pretty tired.

This afternoon we watched a video.

I wonder what we will do tomorrow.